Sticky
Graphic
Novels™
MANLY

MANLY

StickyGraphicNovels.com

Printed and distributed by
ComicMix, LLC.
71 Hauxhurst Ave. Suite B
Weehawken, NJ 07086.
http://www.comicmix.com

Printed in USA.

Hardcover ISBN: 978-1-939888-62-4

MAY 20
FREE TO GOOD HOME
BUDDY
VDOT

BUSTED

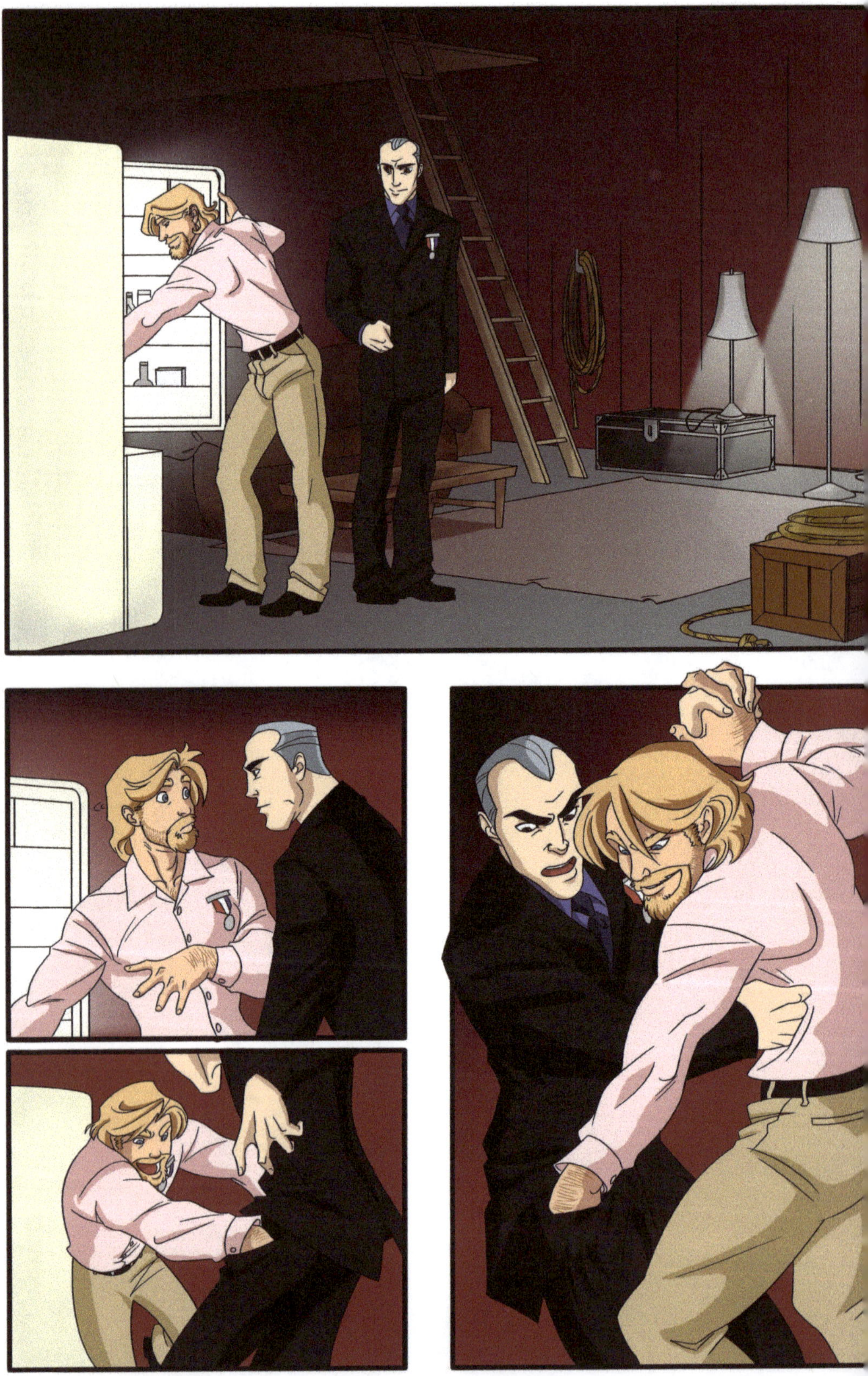

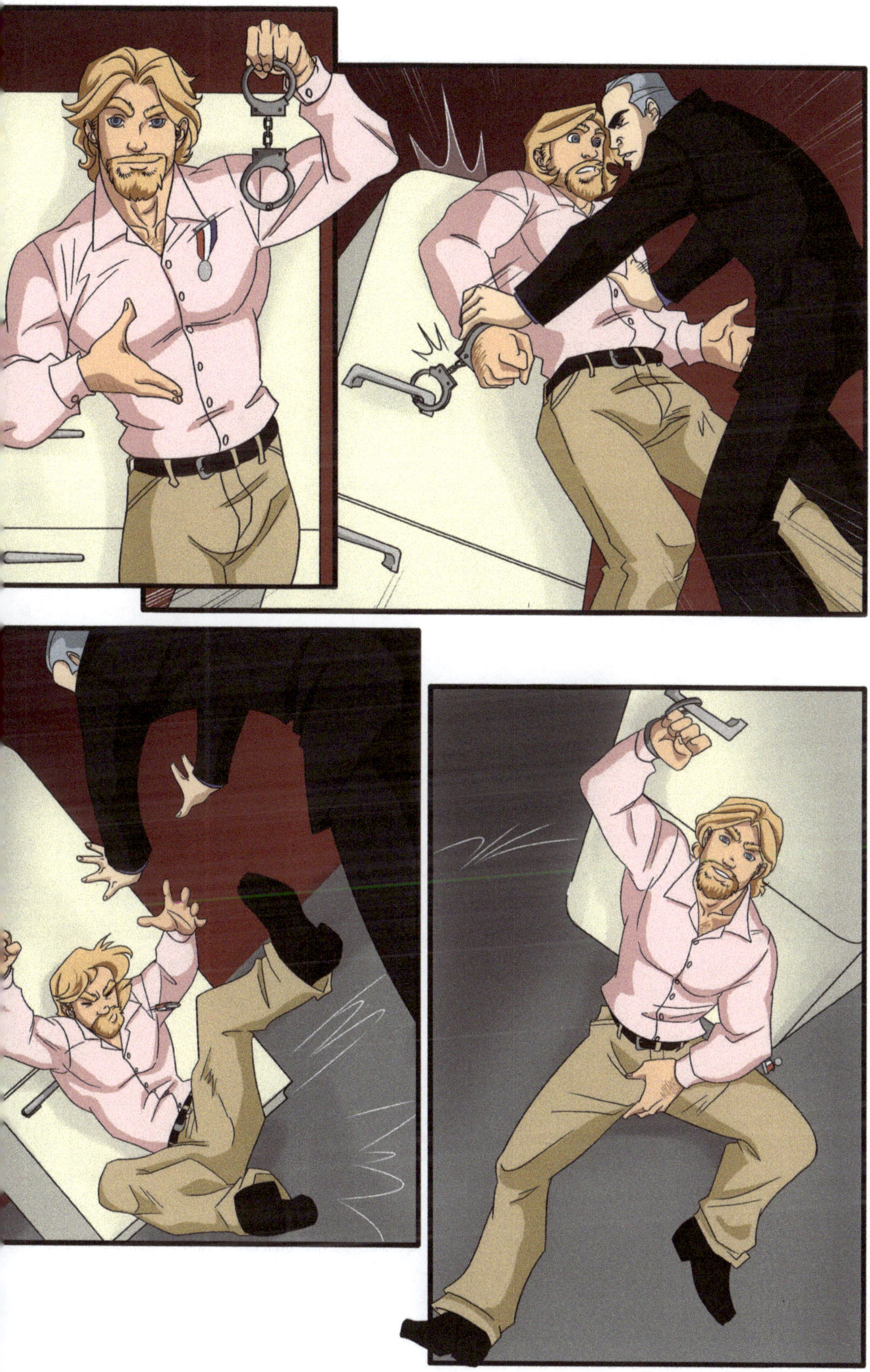

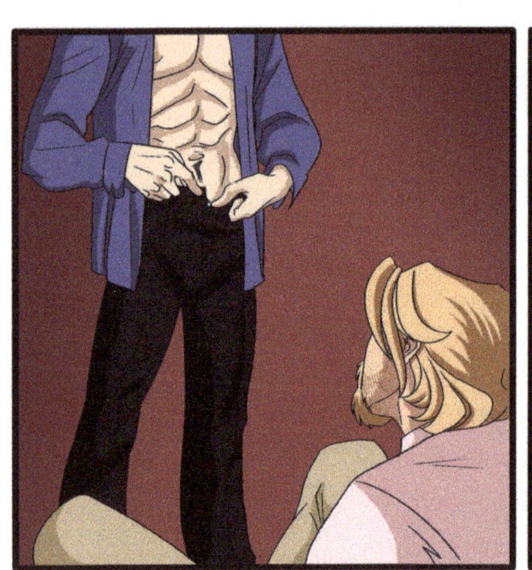

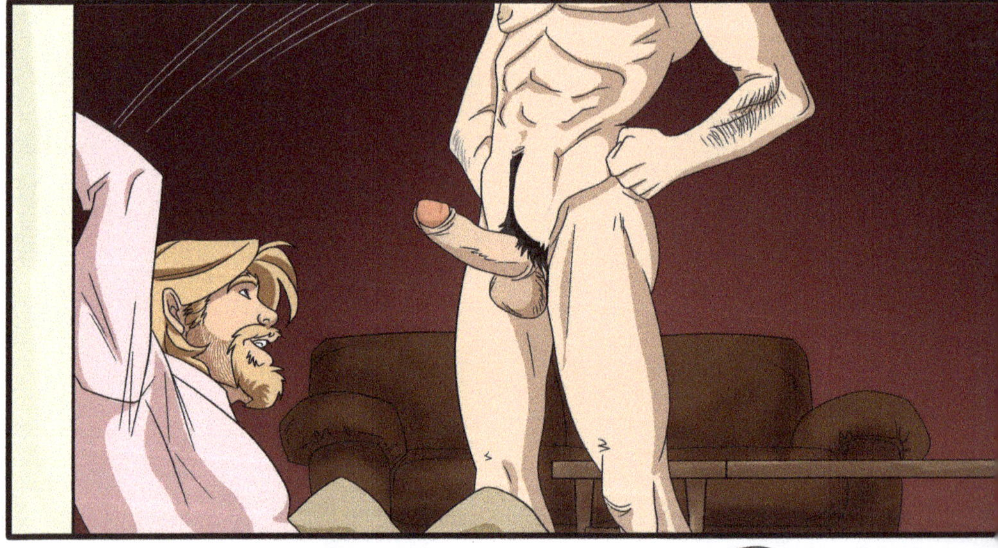

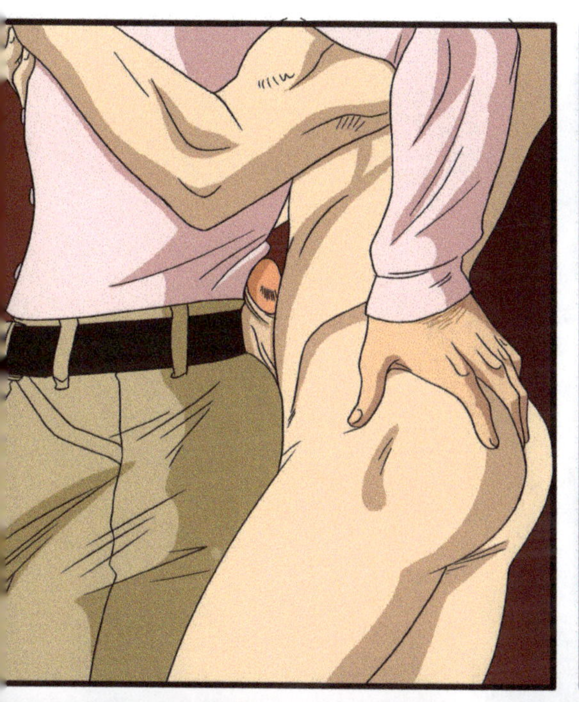

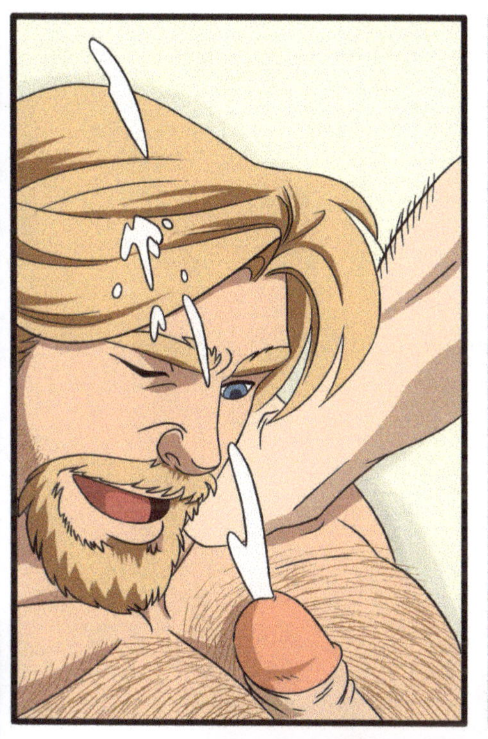

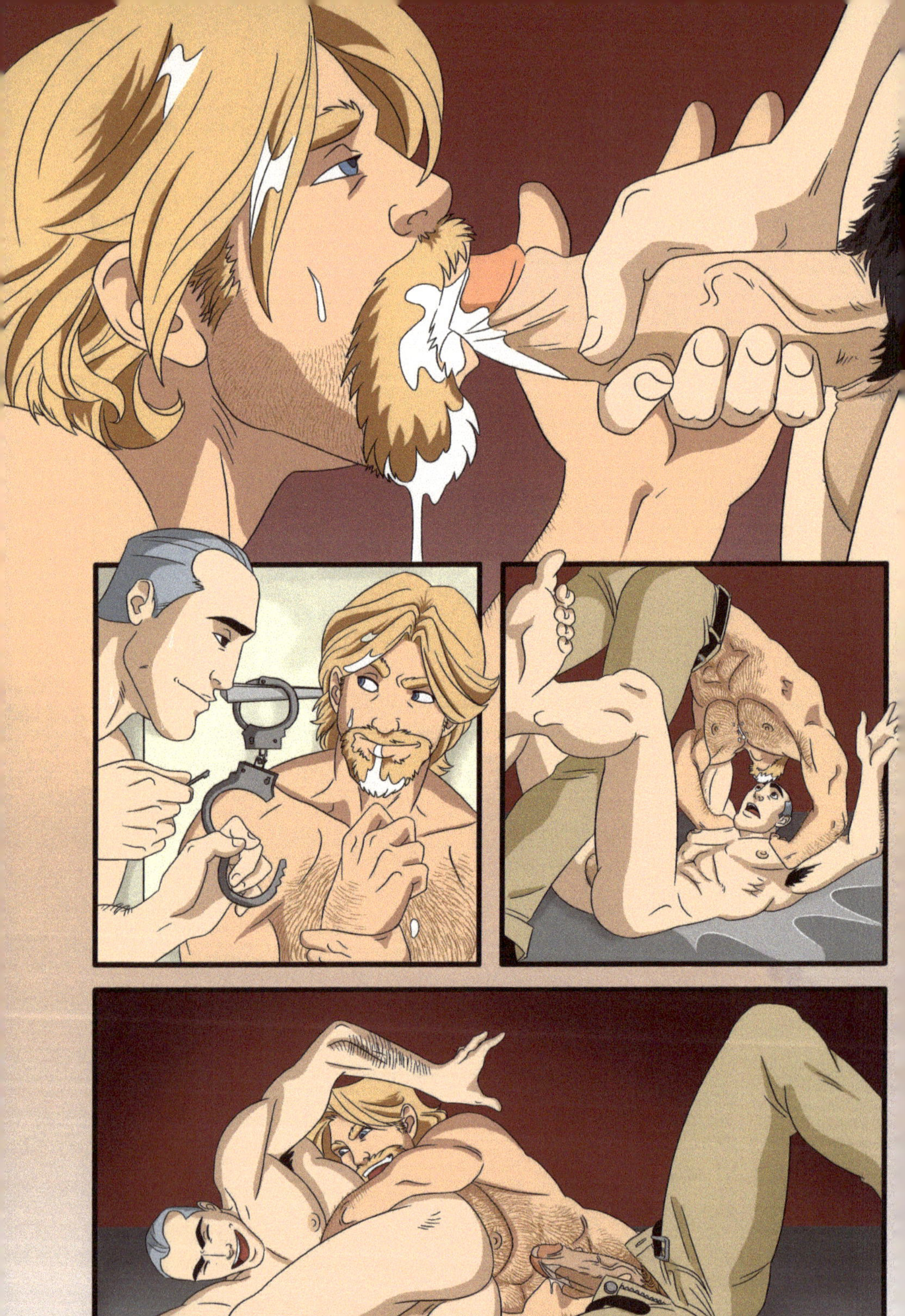

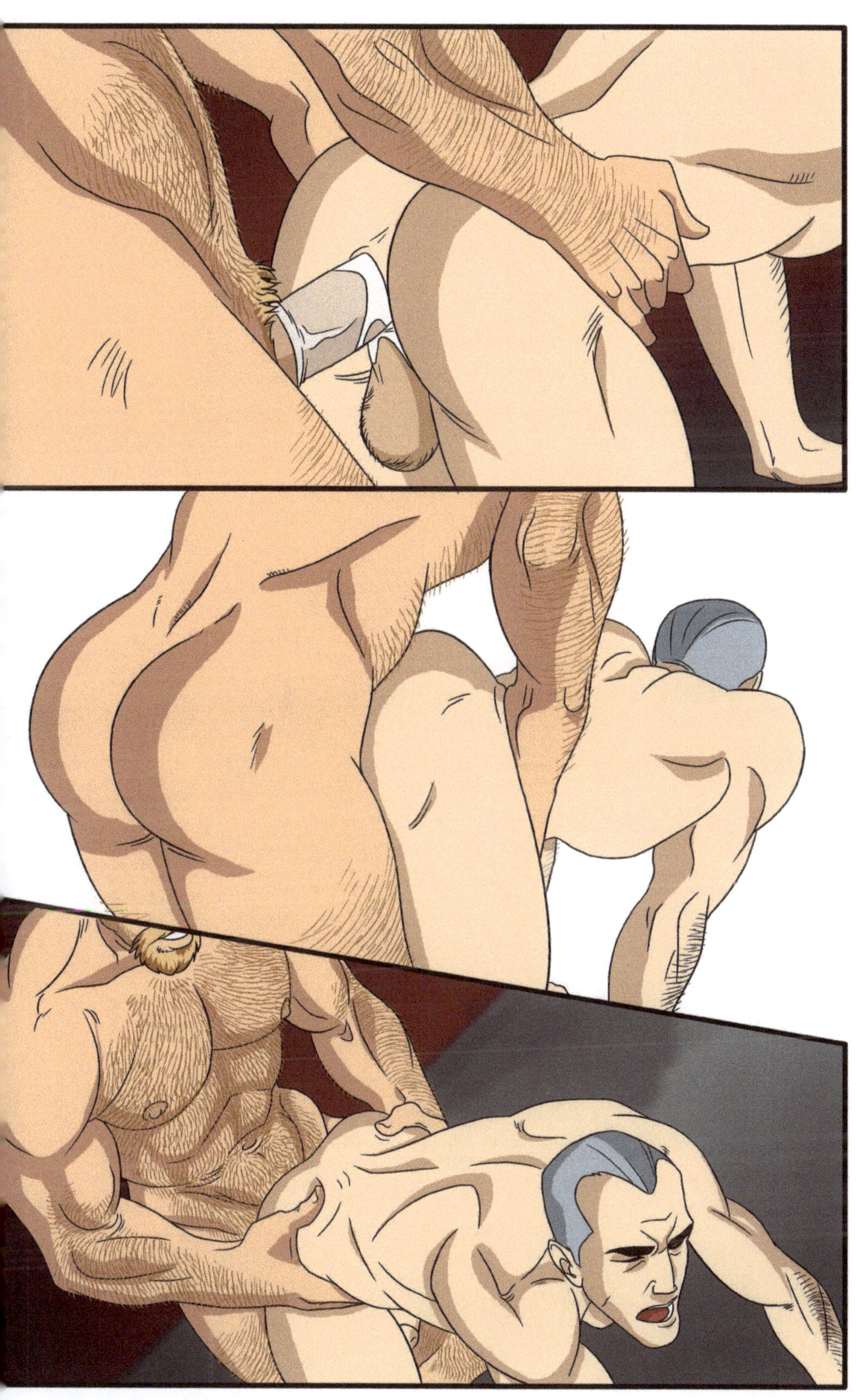

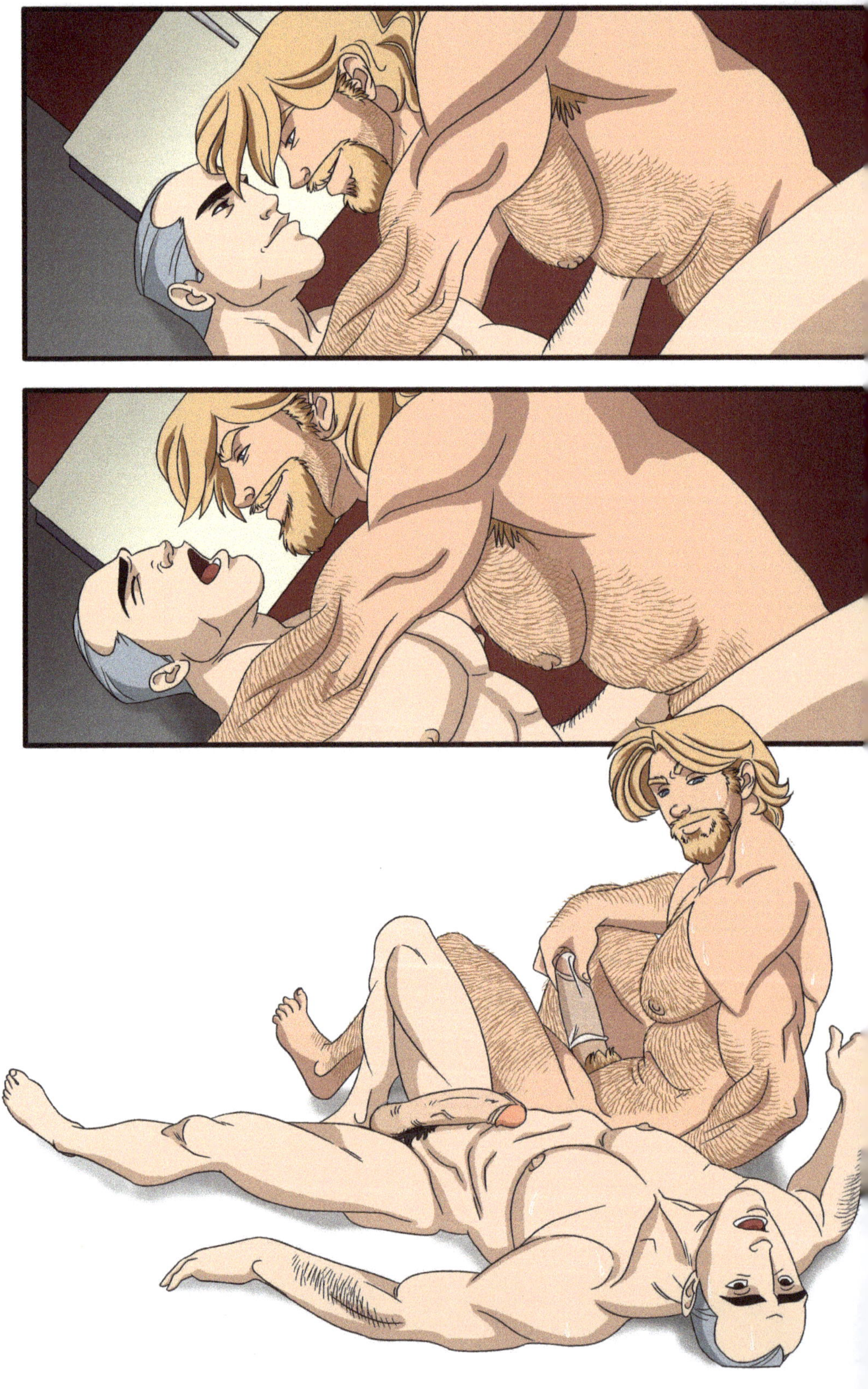

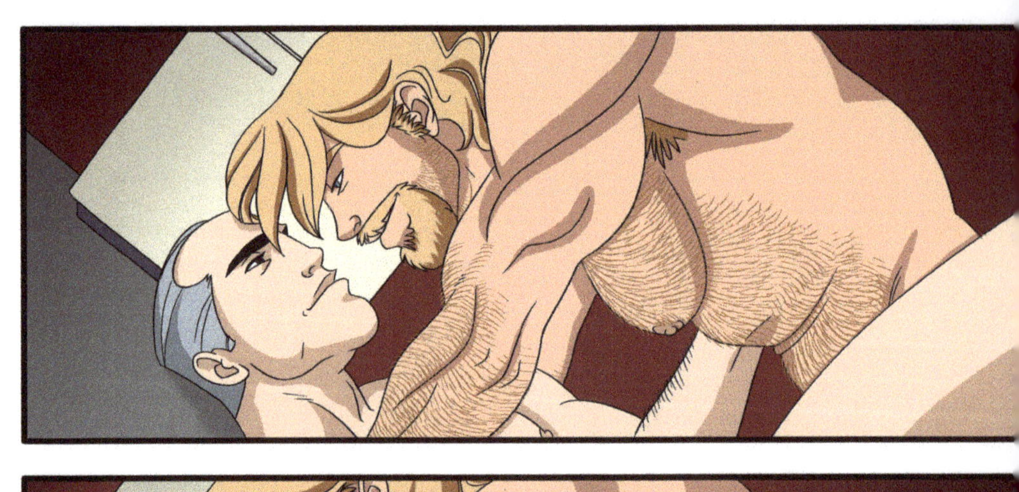

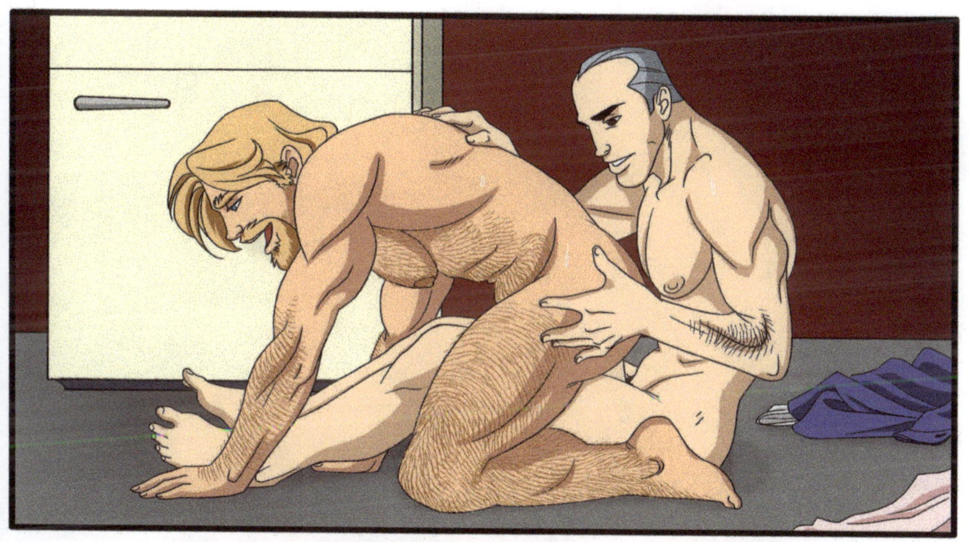

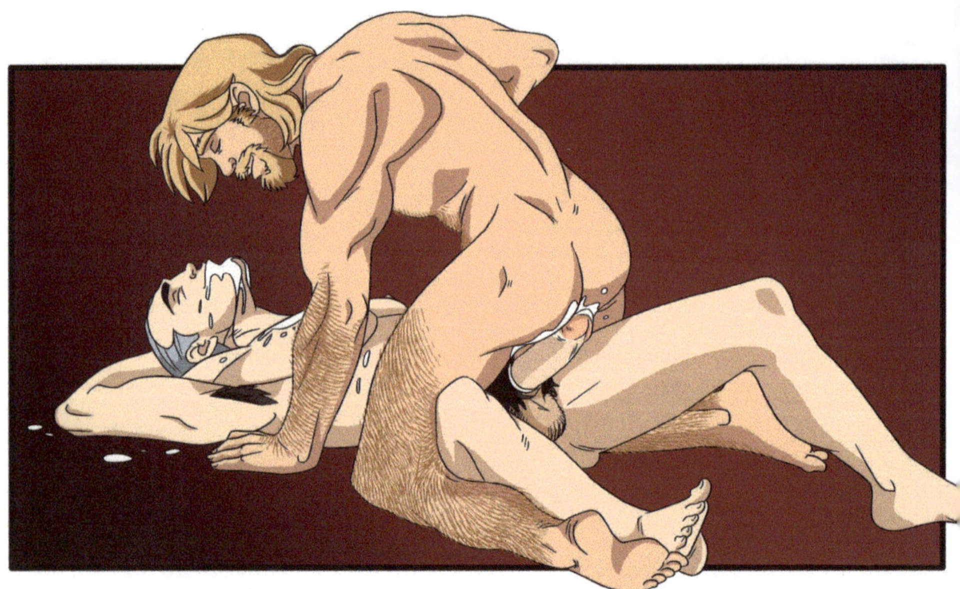

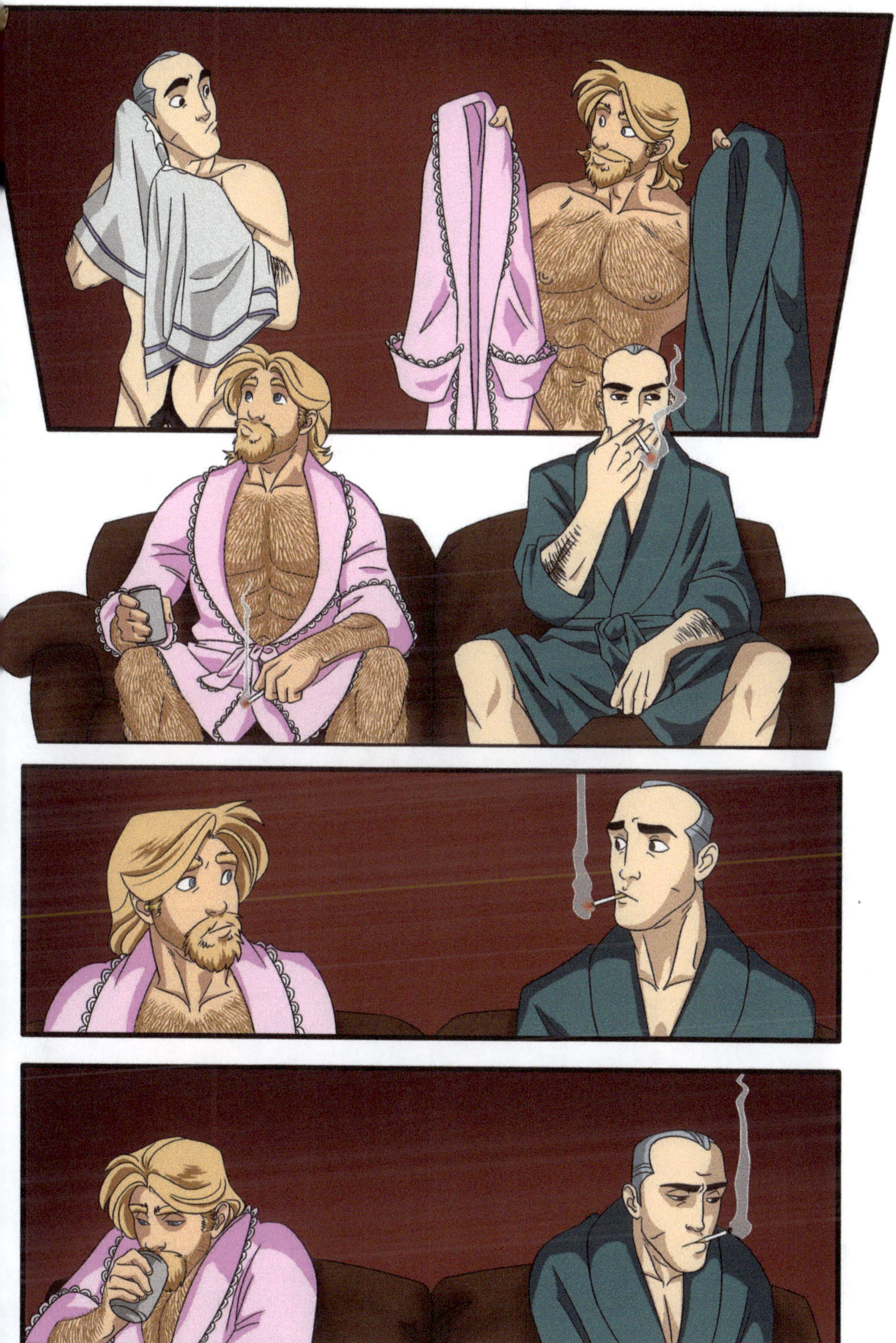

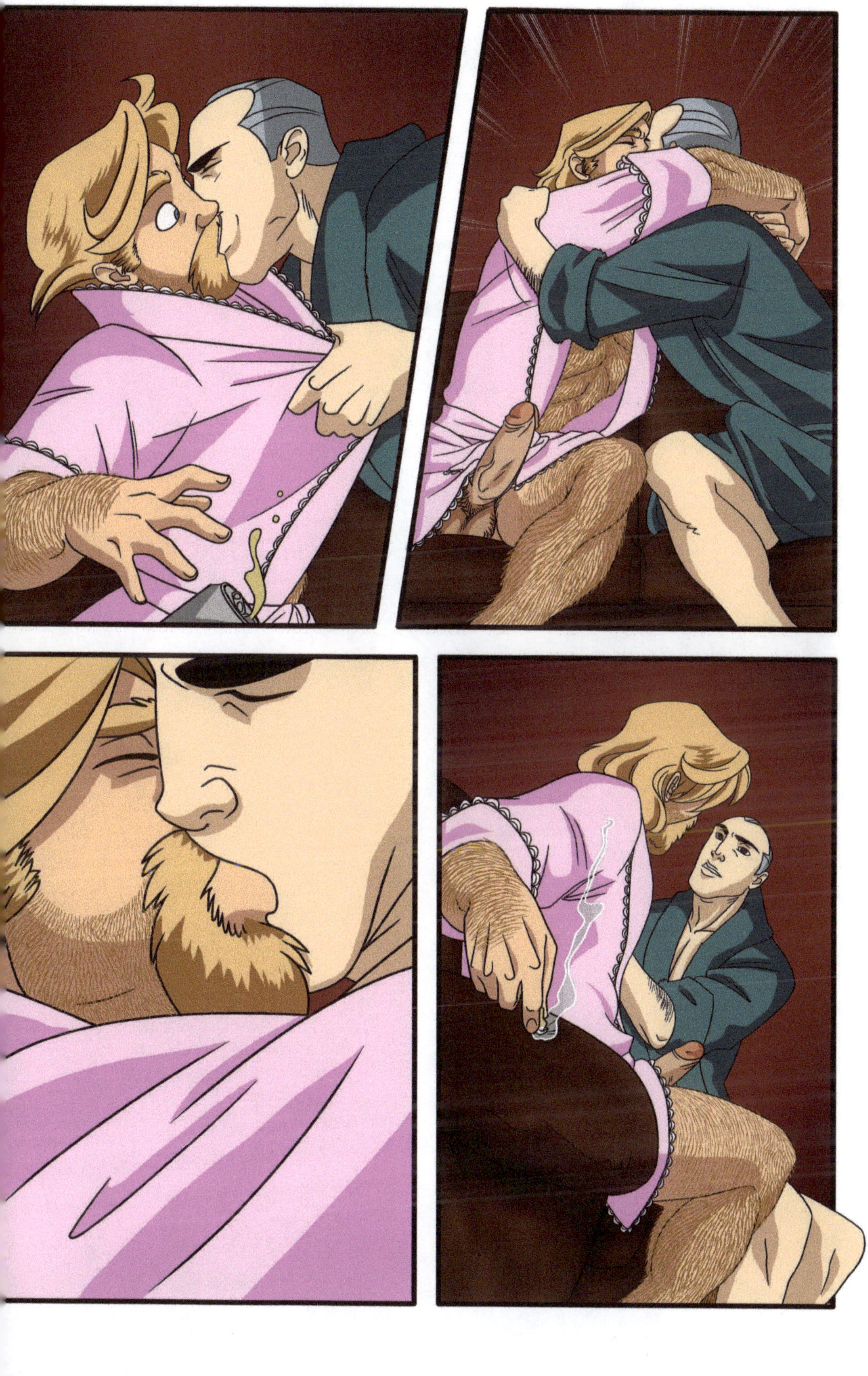

Buster's
BOXING CLUB

BOXING
MAIN EVENT
TONIGHT
KNOCKOUT!
PABLO GUTIERREZ
AMERICAN BOXER

CLINCH

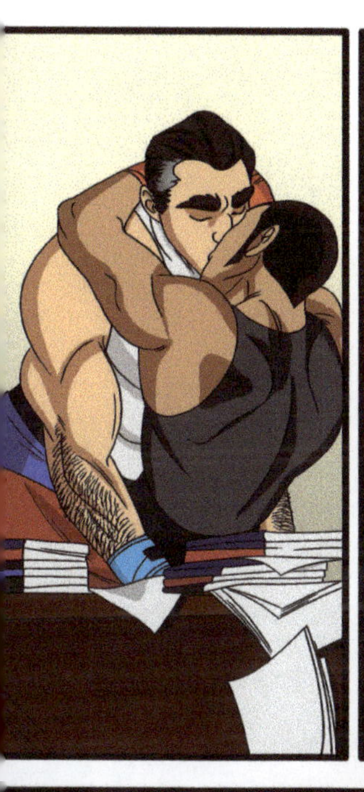

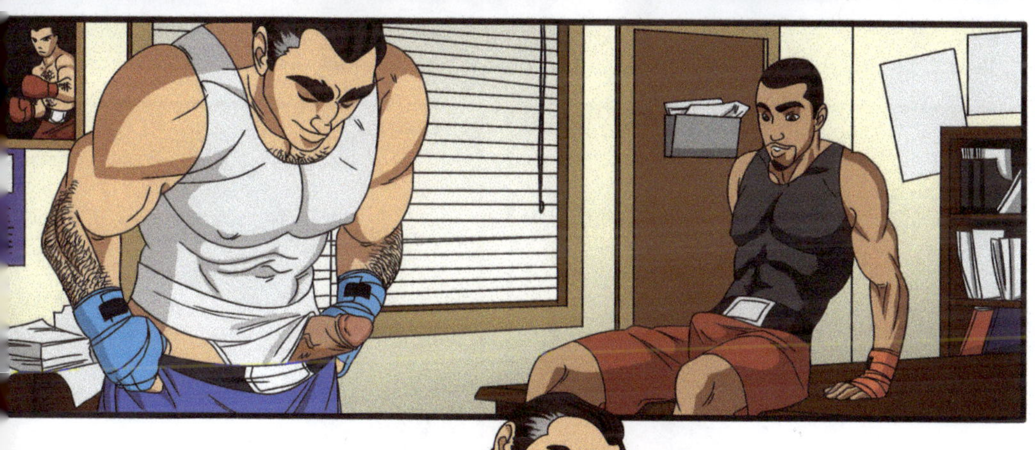

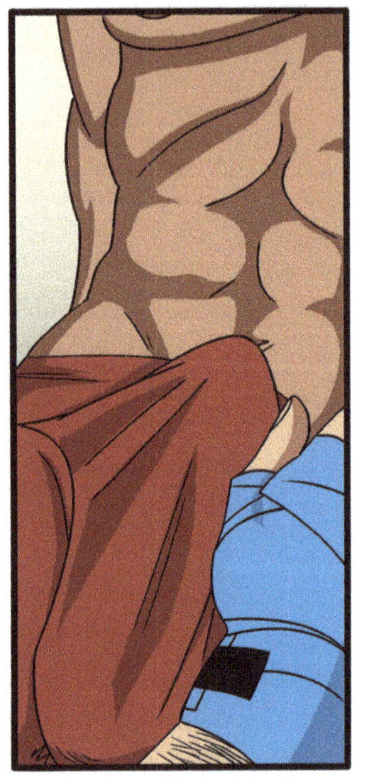
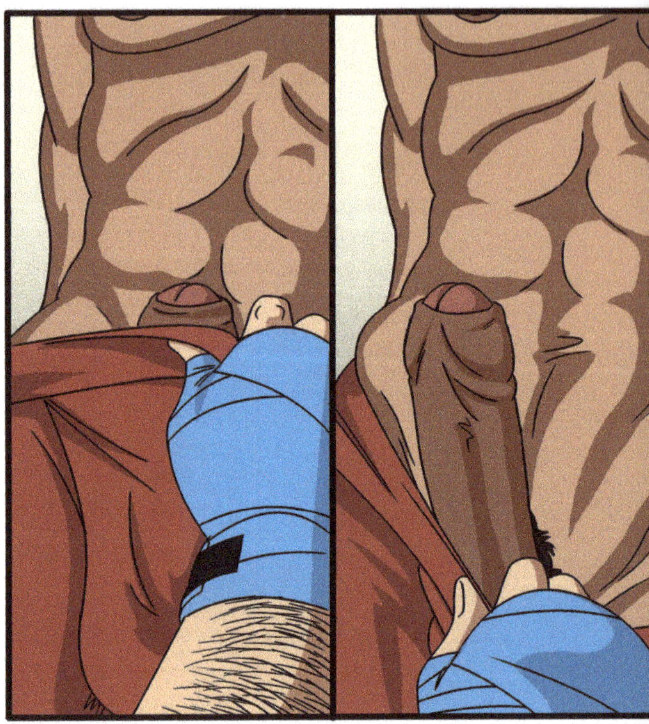

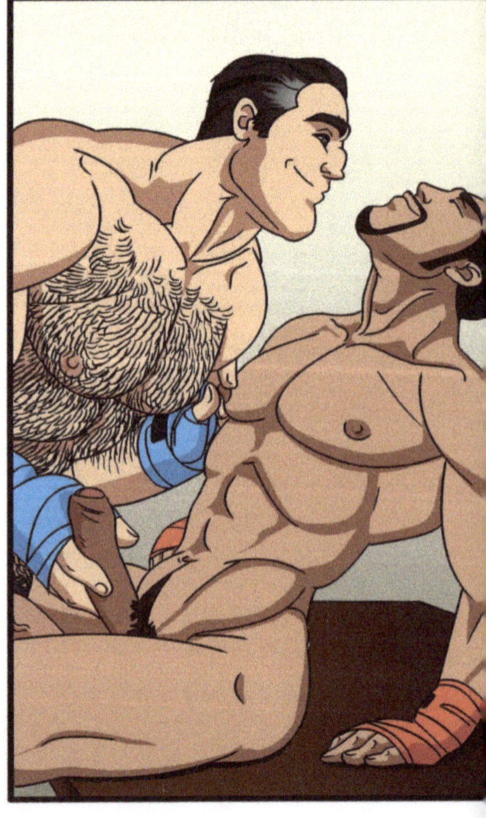

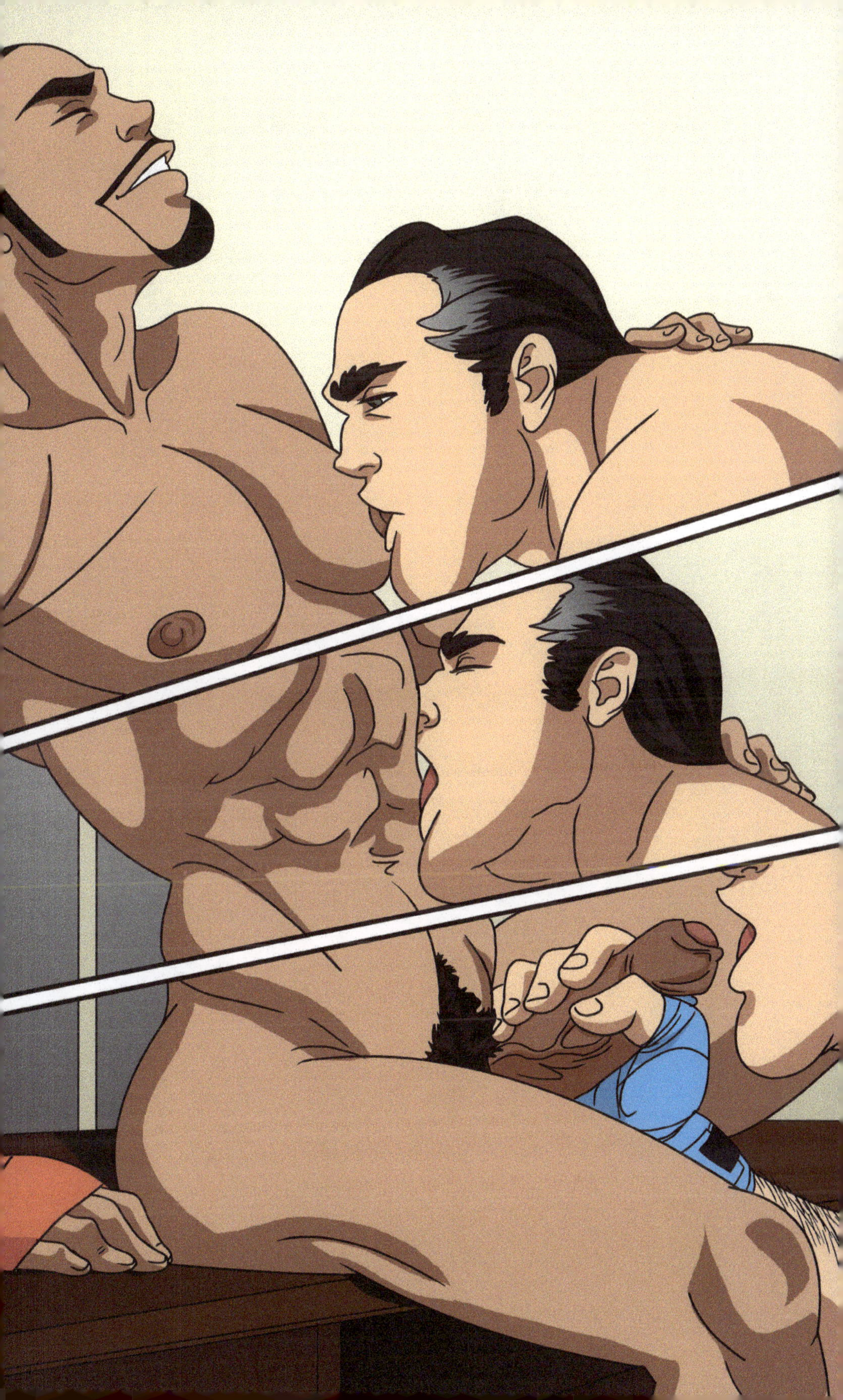

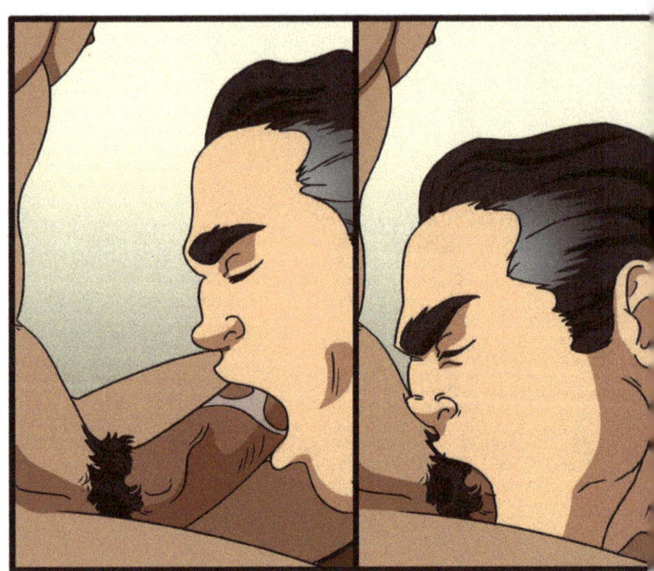

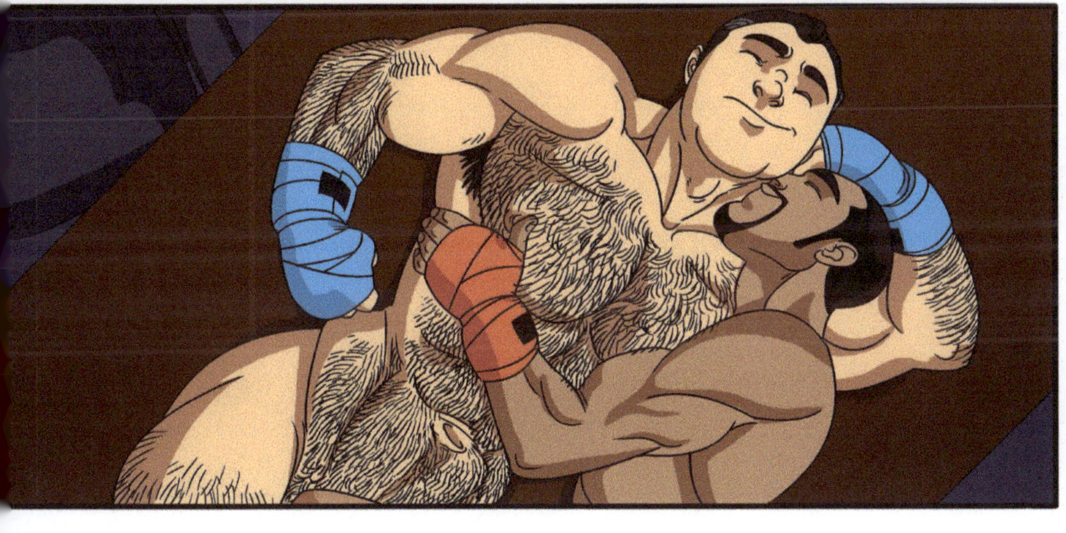

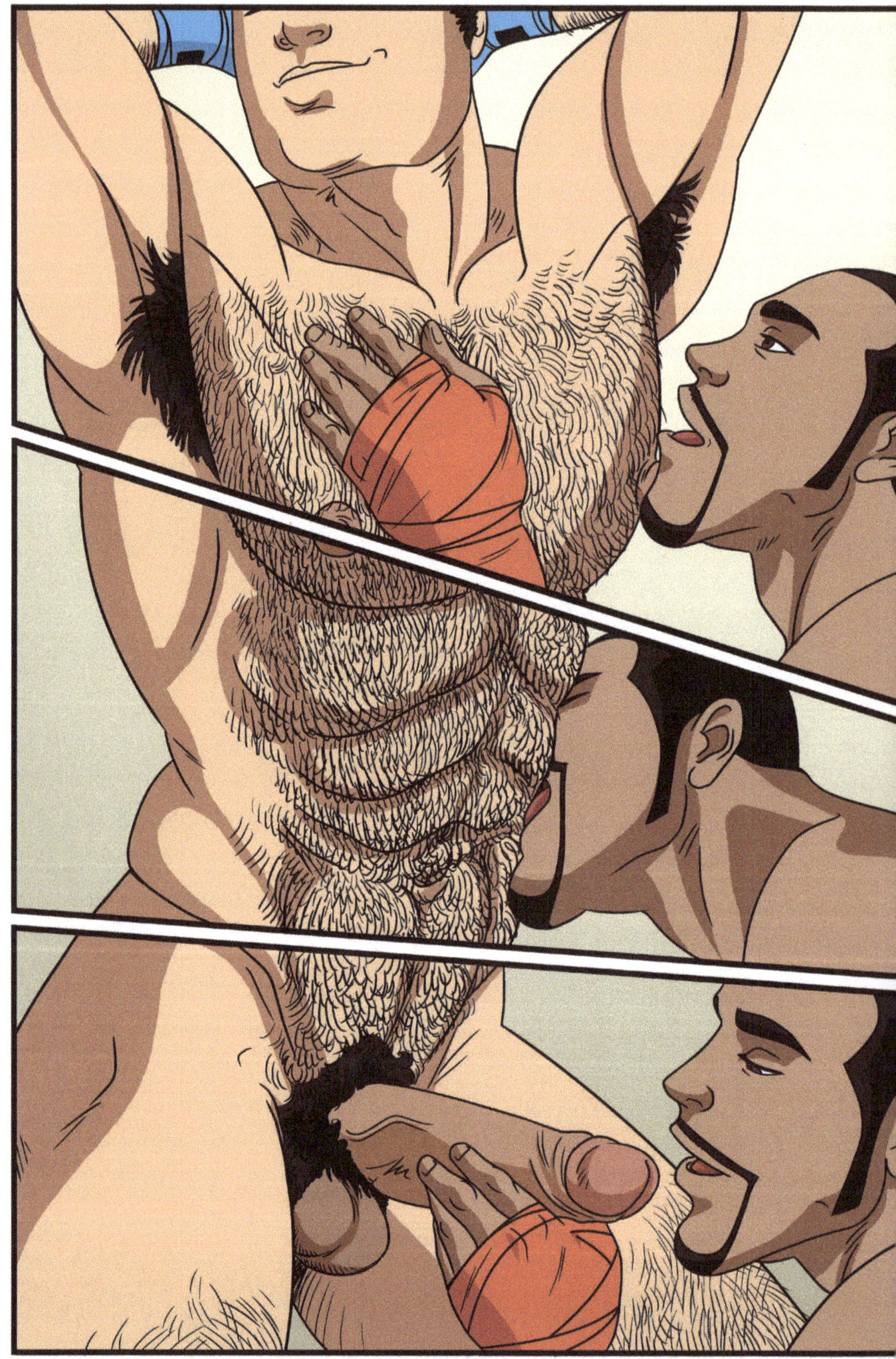

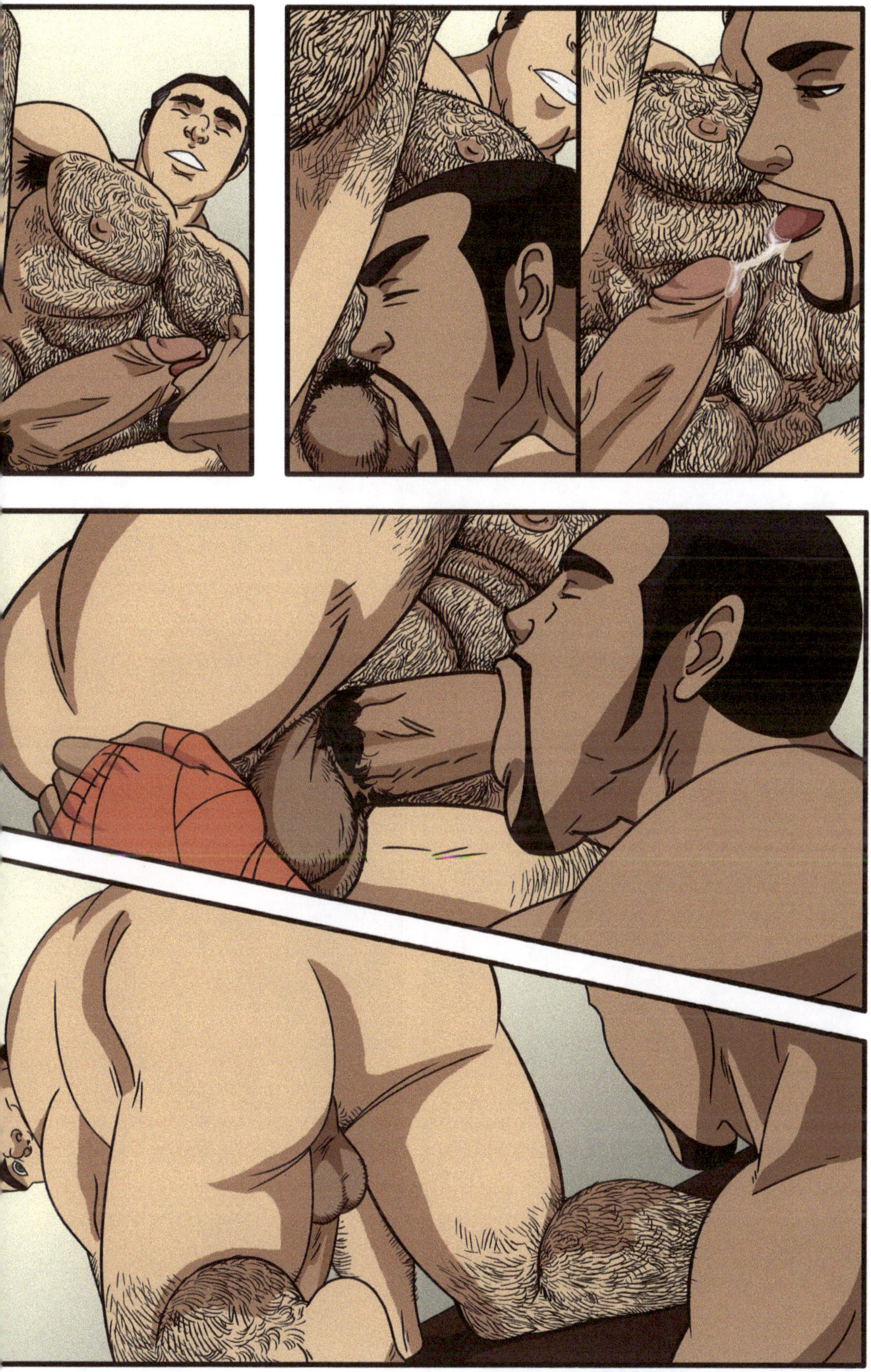

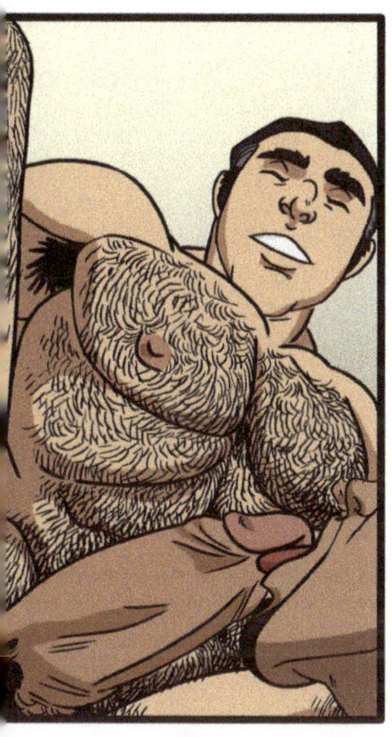

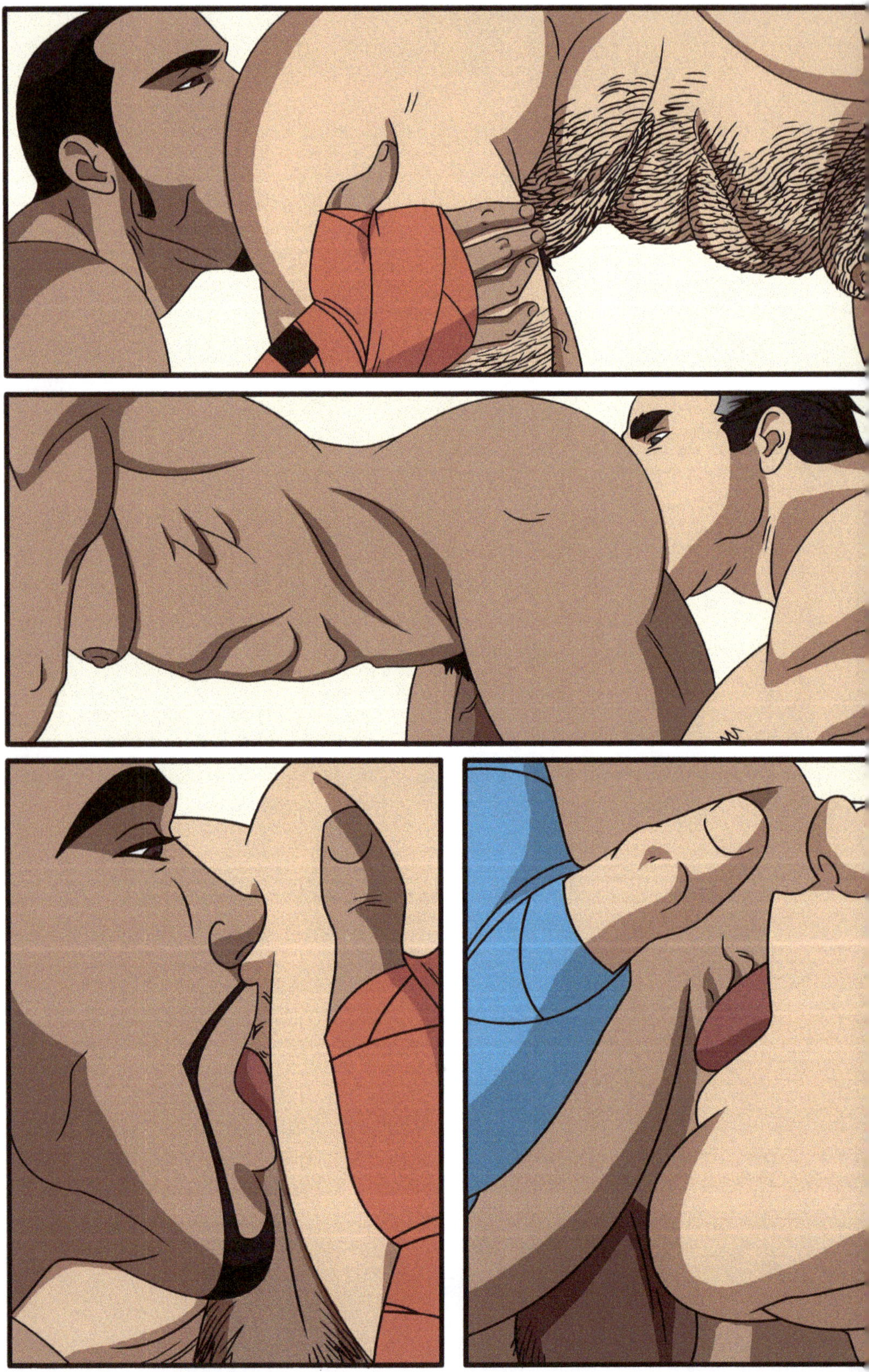

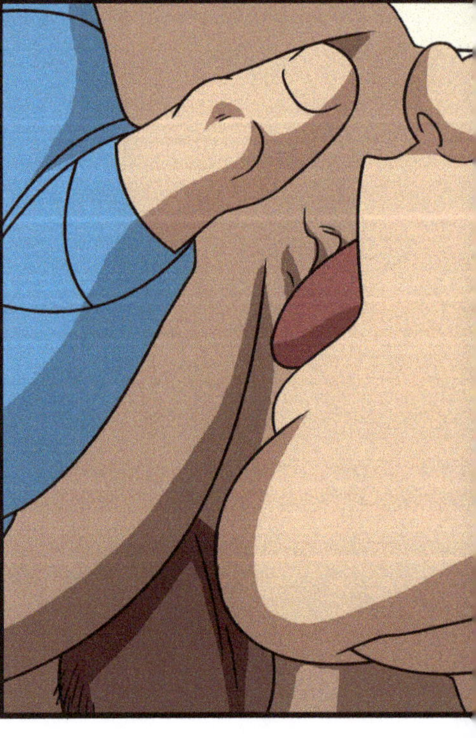

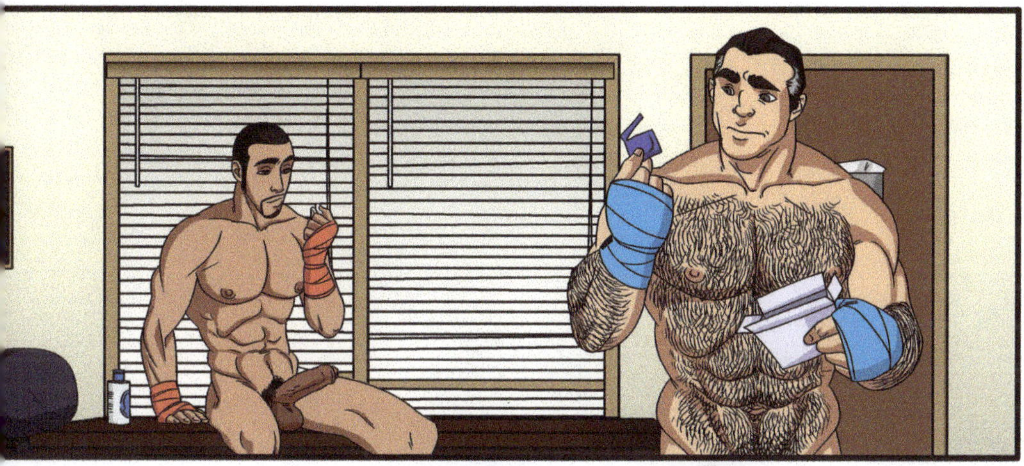

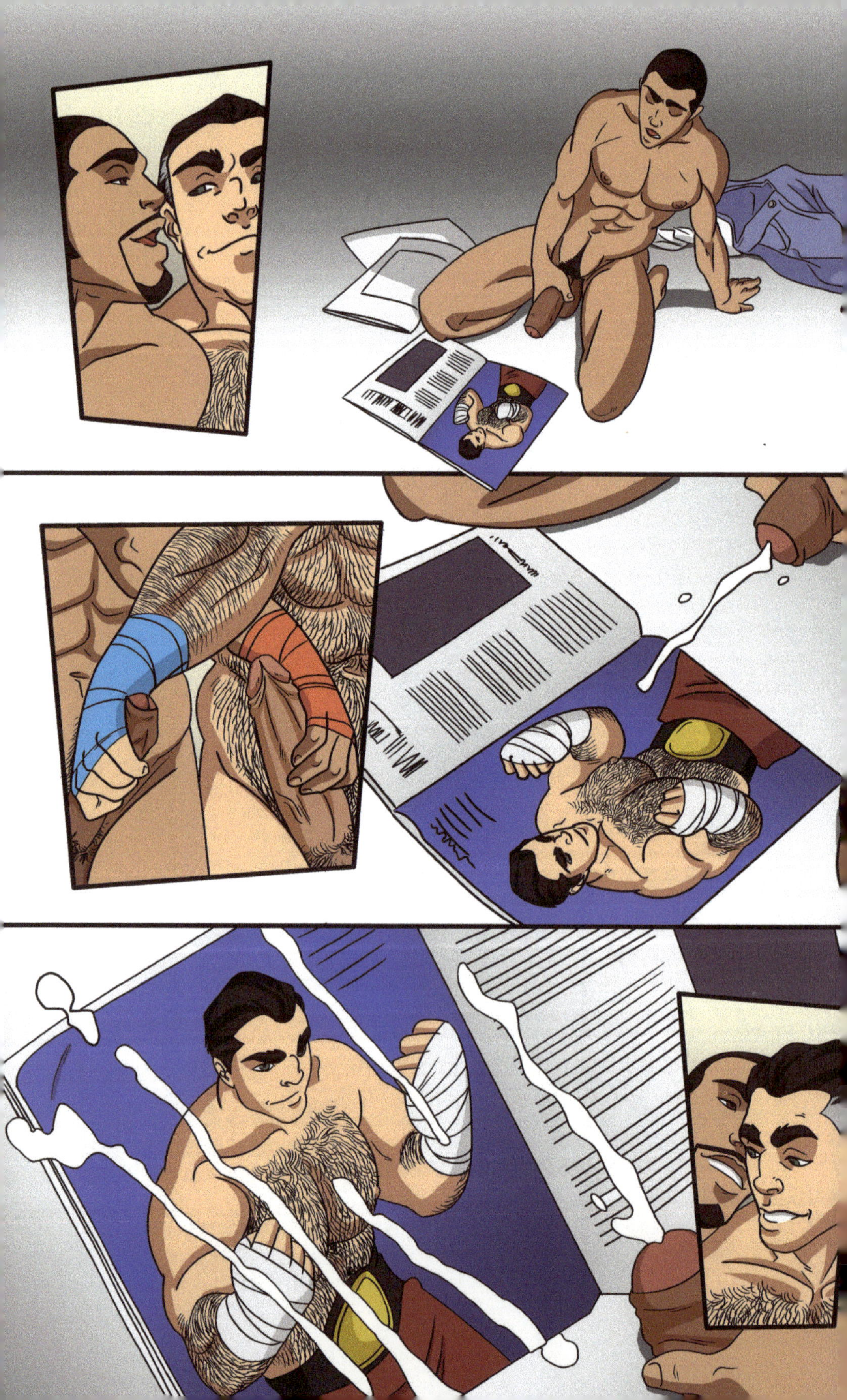

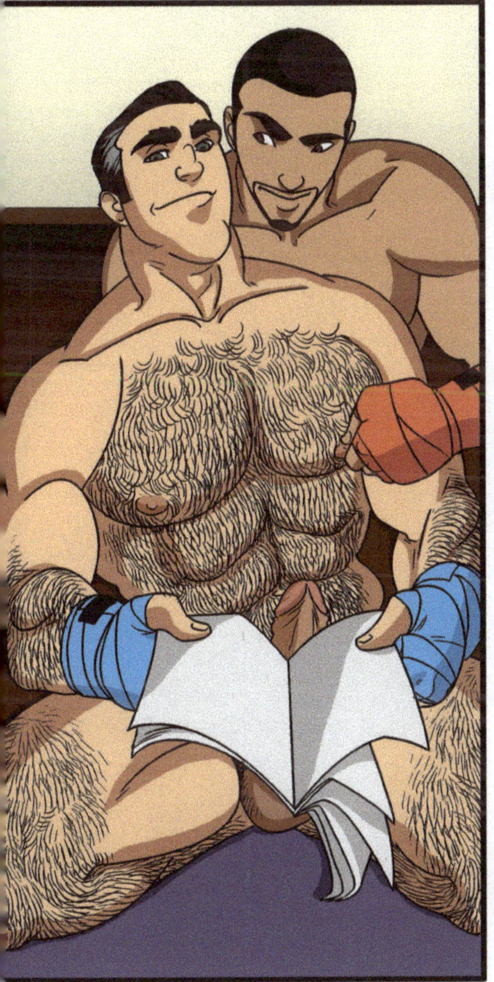

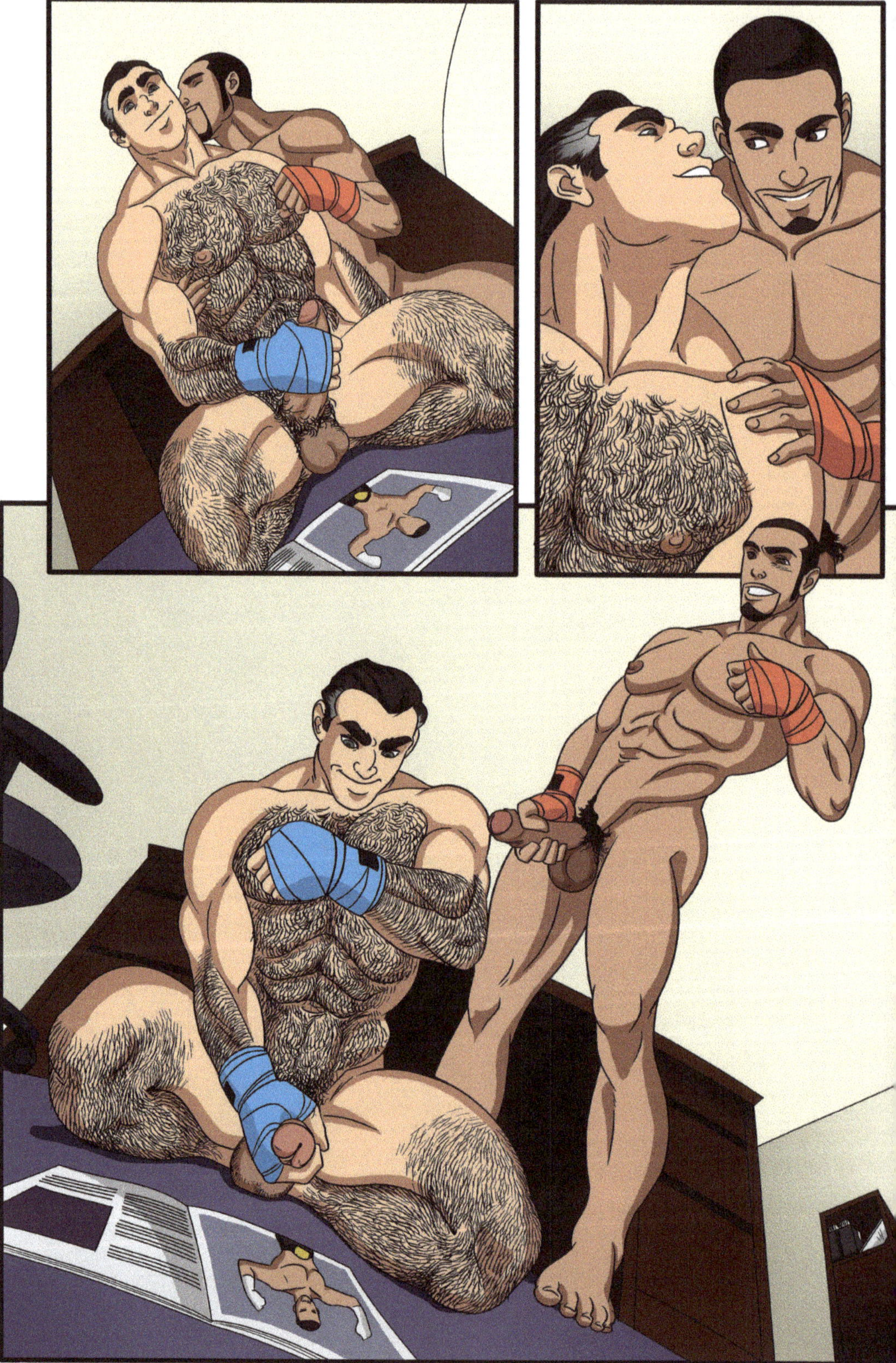

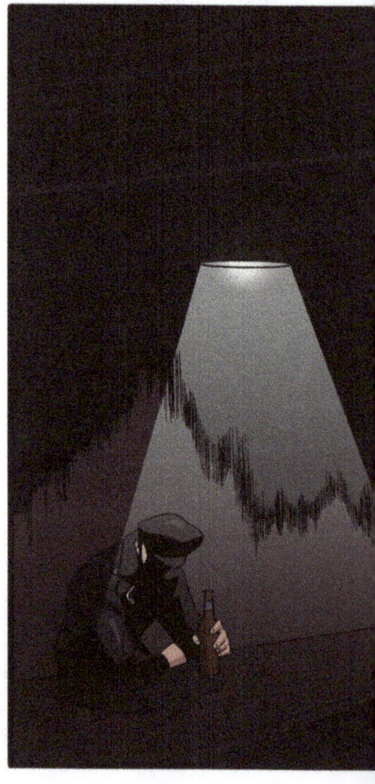

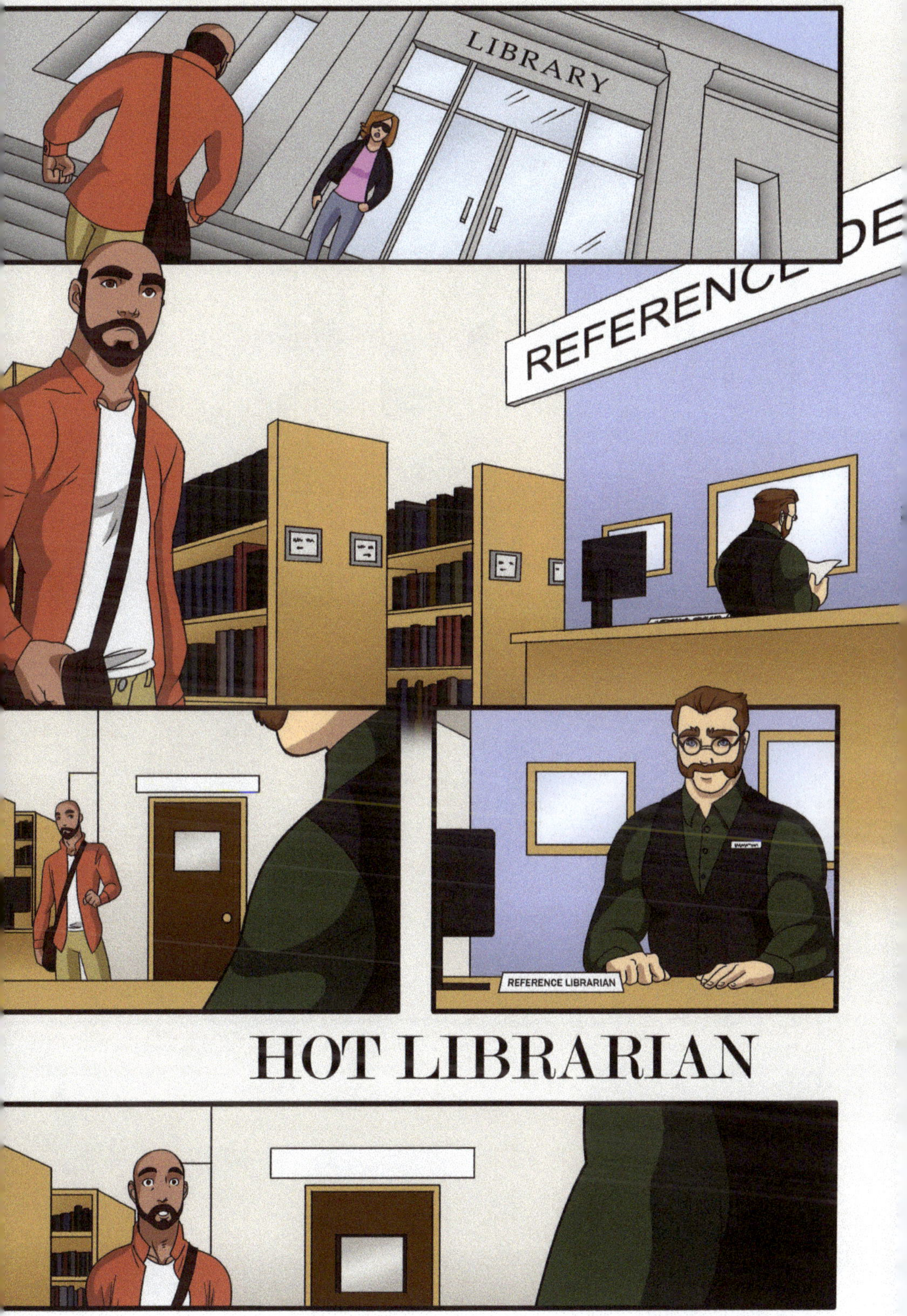

HOT LIBRARIAN

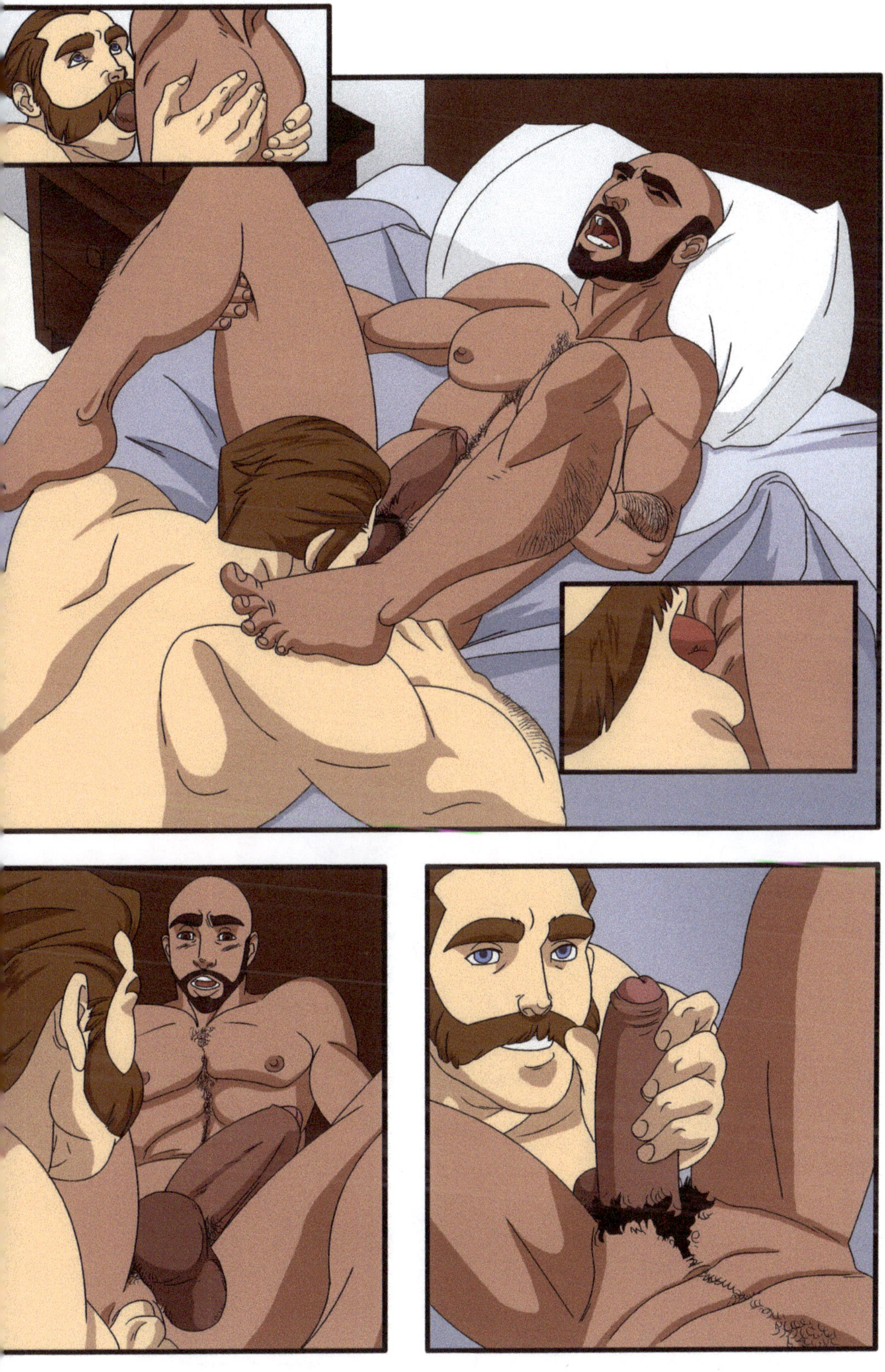

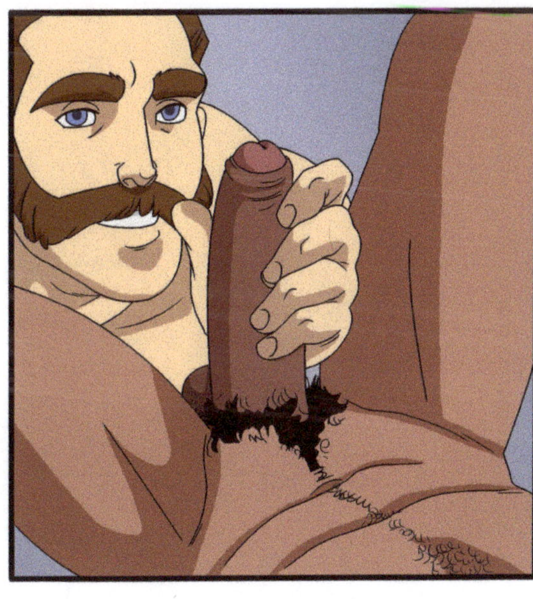

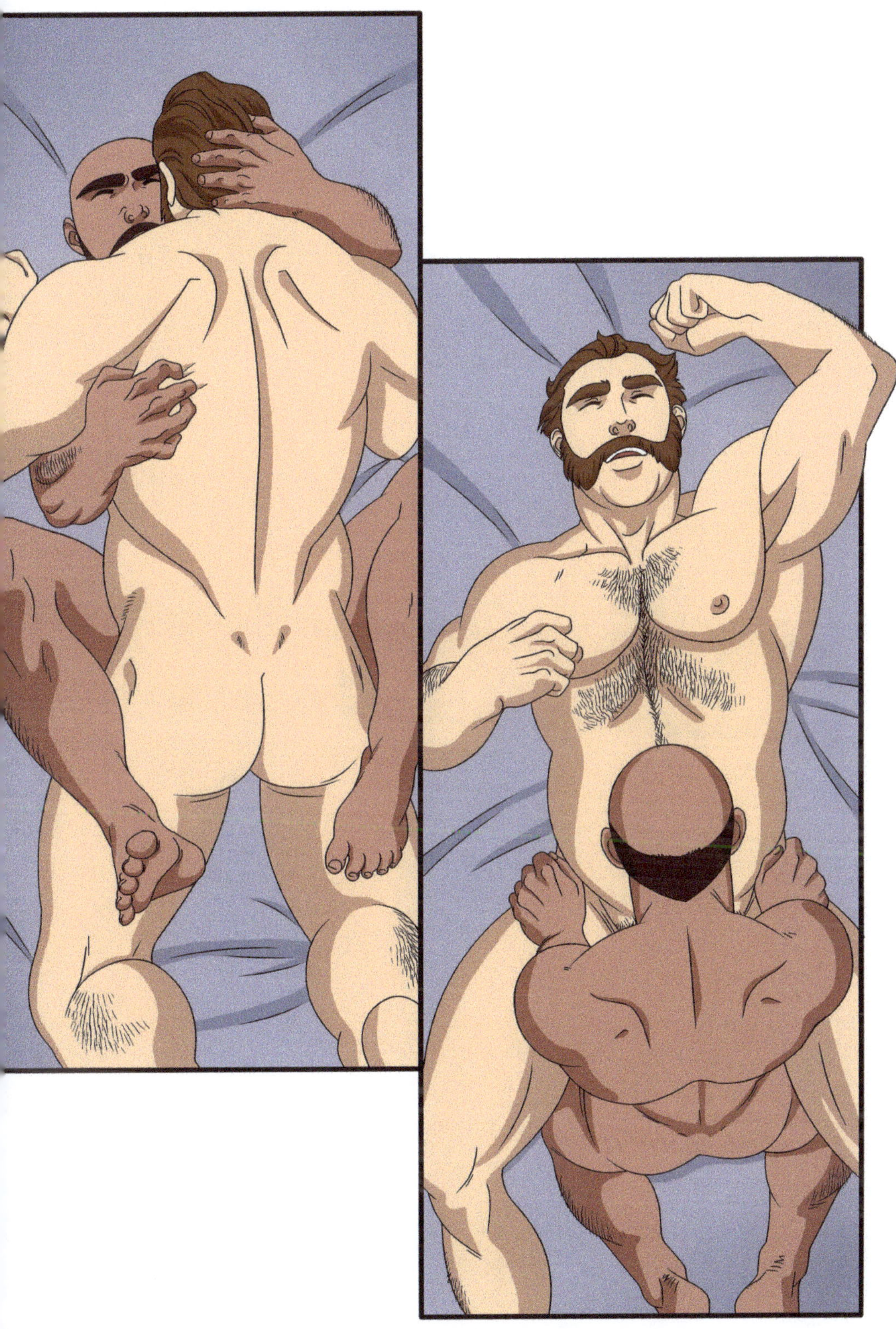

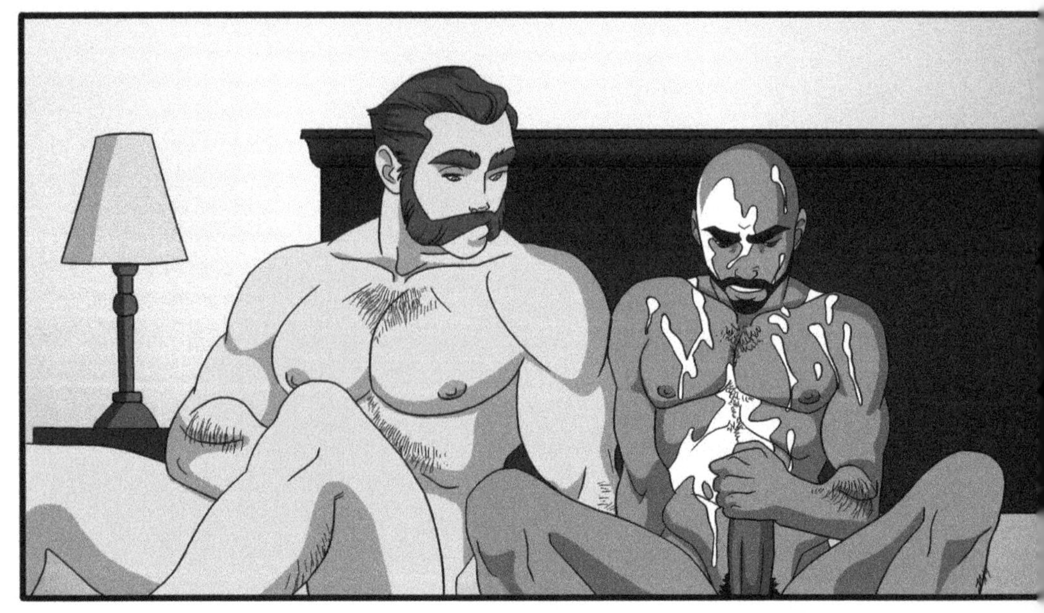

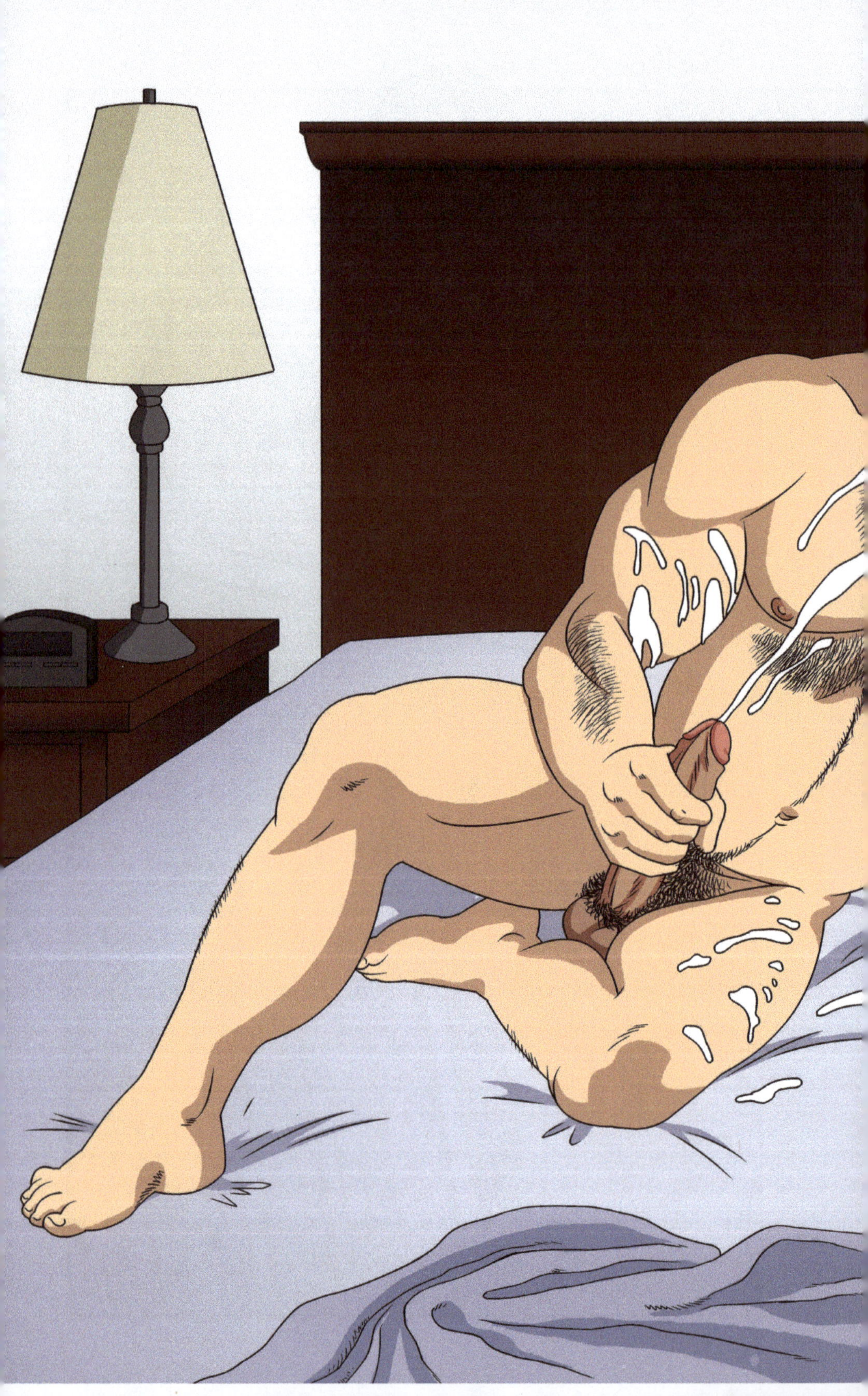

MICHE

About The Authors:

Dale Lazarov is known as The Father of American Bara Comics as the writer, art director and licensor of Sticky Graphic Novels. Sticky Graphic Novels are wordless, gay character-based, sex-positive graphic novels for an international audience that are considered "a joyous expression of male/male sexuality that, while erotic, is neither grubby nor tasteless" (*The Novel Approach*). Since 2006, he has collaborated on 14 hardcover Sticky Graphic Novels and 40 digital editions with distinctive and evocative gay comics artists from around the globe. In his secret identity, he is Aldo Alvarez, Ph.D., and lives in Chicago.

Amy Colburn makes her publishing debut with MANLY after years producing beautiful homoerotic illustrations for a variety of venues. She lives in New York City.

Dominic Cordoba is a digital artist in New Jersey. His site is at dhcunderground. net.

www.ingramcontent.com/pod-product-compliance
Lightning Source LLC
Chambersburg PA
CBHW051120300726
48981CB00002B/196